I0522446

TALES OF ANNWN

Karen Myers

TALES OF ANNWN

THE HOUNDS OF ANNWN

Karen Myers

PERKUNAS PRESS · Tyrone, Pennsylvania

Tales of Annwn

The Hounds of Annwn: A Story Collection

Perkunas Press
2635 Baughman Cemetery Road
Tyrone, Pennsylvania 16686
USA

PerkunasPress.com

Author contact: KarenMyers@KarenMyersAuthor.com
KarenMyersAuthor.com

Cover illustration: Larissa Kulik (Ann Mei)

Trade Paperback
ISBN-13: 978-1-62962-028-2
ISBN-10: 1-6296202-8-9

ALSO BY KAREN MYERS

The Hounds of Annwn

To Carry the Horn
The Ways of Winter
King of the May
Bound into the Blood

Story Collections
Tales of Annwn

Short Stories
The Call
Under the Bough
Night Hunt
Cariad
The Empty Hills

The Chained Adept

The Chained Adept
Mistress of Animals
Broken Devices
On a Crooked Track

Science Fiction Short Stories

Second Sight
Monsters, And More
The Visitor, And More

See KarenMyersAuthor.com for the latest information.

CONTENTS

THE CALL

This story takes place before the events in To Carry the Horn.

In all of her eight years, Rhian had never had a better time out hunting. Her pony Dreinog had kept up with the bigger horses on this gorgeous fall day, and she'd jumped every obstacle that came her way. It was always fun, she thought, but somehow today seemed different, more exciting. It's like I could feel what a good time Dreinog was having, following the hounds.

She hastened to untack him and groom him in the stables behind her foster-father's court. Gwyn insisted that she see to the care of each of her animals, and she enjoyed doing it. Normally she liked these quiet moments after the hunt with her pony, lingering to talk to him all about the adventures they had just had. But this time there was something wrong, something nagging at her. She wanted to find Isolda and talk to her instead. Isolda would know what to do. After all, she was three years older.

She hurried out of the stables and ran to the kennels to look for her friend. Isolda was usually there, helping her father Ives and the other lutins who were responsible for the well-being of the hounds. She found the usual stir of the pack recently returned, the lucky hounds who had been out telling their left-behind packmates all about it, in their own way.

Rhian ignored the noisy hounds, but she was surprised not to see any of the hunt staff. They hadn't come to the stable, either. She ducked her head into the kennel-master's office, and found Isolda there instead of her father.

"What's happened?" she asked.

"Gwennol's missing," Isolda told her. "Iolo brought the rest of the pack home, but he's gone back out with the hunt staff to find her."

Rhian was shocked. She liked Gwennol about best of all the bitch hounds. The young hound had a habit in the field of swooping after the quarry, like the swallow she was named for.

Was that what was wrong, what had been bothering her in the stables?

"Where are they looking for her?"

"Over at Eagle's Nest, where you were hunting," Isolda said. "Where the hounds were last all on together, Iolo said."

"But that's wrong," Rhian blurted out. Something stabbed at her and she cried out. "She's over there," pointing to the southwest, "not back where we were."

"What's the matter with you?" Isolda asked. "Are you hurt?"

"I don't know." Rhian felt a pain in her leg. "I don't think it's me. Maybe it's Gwennol." As she said it, she thought that seemed right.

"How can you know that?" Isolda said.

"I just do," Rhian said, frustrated. "I can't explain it. I'm going to go find her. Come with me."

She didn't think Isolda would do it. She knew this wasn't something the adults would approve of but she couldn't wait. Gwennol was hurt, she was sure of it.

She saw Isolda weighing her choices. The older girl sometimes made her be more careful and she was afraid she'd have to go alone. Despite her years Isolda was no taller than Rhian, the lutins being a short people, and she looked her in the eyes to see if she was telling the truth.

Isolda bit her lip, clearly torn between wanting to help and her informal duty of trying to keep Rhian out of trouble. Rhian tried to obey the rules, most of the time, but this was different. Her foster-father wouldn't want her to abandon one of his hounds.

"Come on," Rhian said. "I'm going."

"Not by yourself," her friend replied, giving in. "Wait for me."

They tried to walk briskly without attracting notice. They presented themselves to the two guards posted at the postern gate that led to the wooded slope of the Blue Ridge mountain to the west.

Rhian looked at one of the guards and said the first thing that popped into her mind. "I lost a riding crop in the woods this morning, and we're going to go look for it." She could hear Isolda's sharp intake of breath at the lie, but Gwennol's distress made her shift from foot to foot in urgency, and the guard took pity on her. It wasn't the first time the girls had used this gate to leave Greenway Court.

As they exited the other side, shivering along the stone walkway through the nasty living hedge that surrounded the court, Isolda said, "We should tell someone where we're going."

Rhian said, "They'll just try to stop us, and Gwennol needs us. They won't believe me if I tell them."

To her surprise, Isolda agreed.

"You believe me, don't you?" Rhian asked.

"I don't understand it," her friend said slowly, "but I don't think you're lying about it."

Rhian was warmed down to her toes by Isolda's trust.

Rhian found the uphill trail to the overlook ledge a trial after a morning of riding. Her legs were wobbly and her feet in their boots were sore, but she could feel Gwennol's pain more clearly as she got closer. Isolda was better shod for the woods path. Rhian looked down at her friend's sturdy shoes in envy.

There was a new note to the hound's distress—not just pain, but fear, too. Rhian was sure something else was there with Gwennol, another animal. She couldn't tell what it was, but she felt hunger and intent. It was after her hound!

"Hurry up, Isolda," she said, and she scrambled as quickly as she could up the trail and paused for breath right on the overlook ledge, with its view of the court. Normally she lingered here, but she hastened on south out the other side.

The hound was close, she knew it. "Gwennol," she called, and the hound began barking in response. The two girls left the trail to cut directly to the sound. The leaves were partially off the trees, and they could see a large animal prowling around a pile of rocks. It lifted its feline head and snarled at them.

Rhian picked up a big stick and so did Isolda. They yelled at the cougar and it withdrew to the far side of the depression between the rocks, a pit that held the trapped hound, her right foreleg bloody and broken.

Rhian tried to throw a rock at the big cat but it barely noticed. She could hear it, it wasn't afraid at all. She felt the hunger and interest in the beast when she looked at Gwennol, and it felt the same when she looked at the two girls. This is dangerous, Rhian realized—we all look like meals to her.

Isolda stood her ground with Rhian. "What do we do now?" she asked. "We can't run away, it can catch us."

Rhian nodded. "She can follow us up a tree, too." She looked down at the hound. "We can't get her out. We'll have to get help."

Isolda said, "Let's start backing away, then."

Rhian looked at her in surprise. "I can't do that. She'll kill Gwennol."

"She'll kill us," Isolda protested.

"No, she won't," Rhian insisted. "I won't let her."

The cougar snarled and started to circle around to their side of the pit.

"Stop that," Rhian said. The big cat stopped. What would happen, Rhian wondered… "Lie down," she told her, sternly. The cougar curled her lip but she lay down along the edge at the top of the pit.

Isolda said, "Send it away, if you can."

"No," Rhian said, thinking about it. "If I do that, she'll come back, and you'll be going for help while I stay here. I can hold her here." I think I can, she said to herself. "Otherwise she might go after you."

Isolda looked very unhappy, but couldn't think of anything safer.

"Tell them to bring rope," Rhian said, "and something to bind Gwennol's leg."

"Don't you dare get hurt, Rhian," Isolda told her insistently. "I'll be as fast as I can."

Rhian listened to the noise of Isolda crashing back through the woods to the trail and settled down to wait. It could take a long time, she knew, an hour or more, before people arrived.

I can't go down into the pit, she thought, because I'm not sure I can get out. She tried to calm Gwennol, partly by speaking to her, and partly with her mind, but the smell of the cougar frightened the hound, and she whined in fear and pain. Rhian felt sorry for her but there was nothing else she could do.

She sat down with her back against a tree to rest her sore feet and talked to the cougar. "Sorry to take your meal away, my lady, but she's a friend of mine. I can't let you have her. Or me, either," she added nervously. "Go find a deer instead."

The cat kept her eyes on her whenever she spoke. The snarl came and went, worse when Gwennol whimpered.

After a little while the big cat seemed to become resigned to her situation and relaxed. Rhian wondered if there were other animals she could hear in the woods around them. She tried to listen in this new special way.

There weren't any deer, of course, not after all the noise they'd made. But gray squirrels above them, safe in their trees, watched, and she felt the field mice in the leaves close to their shelters who weren't paying attention at all. She could feel the sass in the squirrels, taunting the cougar who ignored them.

The whole situation seemed stable, but she thought, it can't last. The cougar will only get hungrier. I just have to hold her off for a few more minutes. I can do that.

The brisk autumn air wasn't waking her up, like she'd hoped. Instead all the exercise she'd had today was making her sleepy. The weight of her head suddenly drooping woke her up in alarm. She mustn't doze off.

It happened a second time, and this time Rhian was startled to find the cougar creeping up on her. She scrambled to her feet.

"Oh, no, you don't," she said. "Lie down and stay there."

The beast snarled and obeyed. It was closer to her now, only a few yards away.

It's taking Isolda a long time, she thought. What if she forgets or something? I've never felt animals like this before. What will happen if it goes away again and the cougar won't obey me anymore?

She forced herself to stand in place and concentrate on staying awake, using the pain of the blisters on her feet to keep her eyes open.

❦

She felt their hounds before she heard them coming, and the two horses, too. They were calling her name, she could hear Isolda's voice.

"Here I am," she cried, "over here."

The cougar looked unhappy at all the noise, and she released her. "Off with you, my lady, and stay out of trouble."

The big cat regarded her steadily, then turned and vanished up the slope. Rhian brushed herself off, and prepared to be scolded.

"We're here," she called again. "The cougar's gone."

She could finally see them as they cut through the woods. Her foster-father Gwyn ap Nudd, Prince of Annwn, was in the lead, on foot, with her older brother Rhys. Behind them were Isolda and her father Ives. Ives had two hounds on leads. Weapons-master Hadyn brought up the rear with two of his guards, mounted.

Isolda ran up to her and hugged her. "I ran to the gate and told the guards. One went to fetch help but the other one refused to leave his post, so I brought my father."

She looked at her father proudly, and Rhian pictured the small lutin with his two hounds holding off a cougar. He must be really brave, she thought.

Ives shrugged. "It's not hard to tree a cougar with a couple of hounds," he said. Her foster-father gave him a look she couldn't interpret.

Isolda said, "By the time we were halfway here, the rest had caught up to us, so I guess maybe the guard was right."

"He followed his orders," Gwyn said, "but if I'd known my foster-daughter would be this reckless I'd have released him to find her."

He turned his gaze on Rhian, and she quavered as she stood there. He never yelled at her, but she hated to have him disapprove. It was so hard to follow the rules all the time. He asked her, mildly, "Where's your cougar, young lady?"

She answered him forthrightly. "I sent her away when I heard you coming."

Rhys called over from the pit. "Here are her tracks."

Gwyn looked hard at her, and she stamped her foot in exasperation. "Nothing happened. Punish me later. Get Gwennol out, she's hurt."

Gwyn raised his eyebrow, but to her surprise, he turned from her and sent Ives and one of Hadyn's men into the pit. They bound the hound's leg to a stick as an impromptu splint, and hauled her out to safety.

There was more noise downslope from them, and she saw Iolo ride up through the trees from the south, with Thomas Kethin and the hunt staff. Isolda told her, "They sent Thomas Kethin to find Iolo, too."

Iolo took in the scene and bowed formally to Rhian. "Thank you, my lady, for your care of my hound."

She didn't know what to do in response to the unexpectedly serious words from the huntsman, so she bowed in her breeches and boots, and hoped that would be alright.

Gwennol's relief in the care of her familiar kennel-master and the easing of some of the pain echoed in Rhian's head. "Oh, she feels so much better," she cried. Her lower lip quivered and she tried not to burst into tears. She was so tired.

Her foster-father walked up to her and wrapped one arm around her, his open jacket like a cloak. "Hush, now," he said. "You did a very brave and a very foolish thing. I'm glad you weren't hurt. We all are."

She stood enveloped in his warmth and sheltered from the world. He didn't do this often, he was so formal. She must have really worried him, she thought, and hiccuped.

She stopped sniffling and spoke into his chest. "I didn't think you'd believe me, sir, when I said I could hear Gwennol calling."

"We'd have been surprised, but we'd have believed you. You heard the cougar, too, and stopped her from chasing Isolda?"

She nodded. "I didn't want you to hurt her, she wasn't doing anything wrong. That's why I sent her away when I heard you coming and I knew she wouldn't want to stay."

Gwyn released her, and she saw Rhys listening, too.

She asked her brother, "Can't everyone hear the animals, once they're old enough?"

"It's called the beast-sense," Gwyn said. "Not many of the fae have it, and not many show it this young."

He looked down at her sternly. "Next time, tell someone. Don't go off like this on your own."

"I wasn't on my own," she protested. "I had Isolda with me."

"And what if any harm had come to her?" Gwyn asked.

Her mouth opened but she was speechless. She hadn't thought of anyone else, and hung her head.

Ives said, "Be glad the hound was found and no one was hurt. Isolda should have known better than to let you do that."

Isolda protested, "But who can stop her?"

Rhys laughed, and even Gwyn chuckled. Rhian was indignant. They're making fun of me, she thought. Still, she was glad it was over and she didn't really seem to be in trouble.

Iolo sat on his big horse, with the bandaged hound cradled before him, and someone gave her a toss up to one of the guard's horses.

She listened to Gwennol's relieved mind and then marveled at how high up from the ground she was sitting. She couldn't reach the stirrups, but the guard was leading the horse anyway so it hardly mattered. She'd never come off a horse for a little thing like no stirrups, anyway, and besides, she could listen to him as he walked, now. I bet I can hear Dreinog, too, she thought.

Something struck her before they started off. "Does this mean I can do what Iolo does? Hunt the hounds?" she asked Gwyn.

Iolo stared at her, and Rhys rolled his eyes.

There was a pause. "We'll see," her foster-father said.

She hung her head again. That means no, she thought.

Ives said something to Gwyn.

"But you can help in the kennels, if you like, for a start," Gwyn said.

"Yes, please! Thank you." The whole day seemed brighter, as if the sun had broken out of the clouds.

She beamed at them all as they headed back to the postern gates.

UNDER THE BOUGH

This story takes place between To Carry the Horn and The Ways of Winter.

"I haven't lived with anyone for hundreds of years," Angharad said. "I'm much too set in my ways, too used to living alone."

Her old friend Tegwen looked at her pointedly in recognition of the feebleness of these excuses.

"You'll adapt," she said.

But do I really want to, Angharad wondered.

"What do you think of George? Truly?" Tegwen prodded.

She couldn't help it. Her face warmed and she smiled affectionately. She glanced around the morning room to see if Tegwen's husband Eurig was in sight, but he must be outside seeing to the running of his estate. They were her oldest friends. They had come to the new world in exile together, when Gwyn ap Nudd, Prince of Annwn, had transferred his domain.

She owed her honesty. "He's kind, bold, even… ardent." She looked at the floor. "He makes my knees melt."

And makes me laugh, too. But was that enough?

She voiced her deepest fear. "He must think me a dried out old lady," she whispered. "He's so young."

"And his age bothers you?"

"Not by itself, no, but we hardly know each other."

Tegwen asked directly, "Do you have any doubts of him?"

"No." It was true, that wasn't the issue.

"But what about the short life?" she continued. "You know his background and there's hardly any fae in him at all. And Cernunnos, the god he carries, who's to say that will lengthen his life? In fifty or sixty years, he'll be gone."

"Cai only lasted fifteen years after you married, and he was as much of a fae as anyone," Tegwen said, bluntly.

"The life of a paladin," Angharad agreed.

She would be taking him up, she thought, and giving him a place in her heart only to lose him again. It hurts too much, afterward. And then Cai, Cai was gone all the time at the end. George is nothing like Cai. He's human, mostly, not some sort of champion. Cai had become hard and grim before he was killed. At least George will be spared that.

Deep down, she admitted it—he already had a place in her heart. It was too late to avoid that.

"What about Cernunnos?" she said. It embarrassed her to talk about it. "It's one thing to sketch him in his manifestations. It's another to… trip over him in the morning. It's George I'm marrying, not the beast-master god. I won't have it. No privacy."

Tegwen half-smiled in sympathy. "Did you speak to George about it?"

Angharad looked away in remembrance. "He said the strangest thing. He said, 'he'll have to answer to me.' As though he could stand up to the god."

"Maybe he can," Tegwen said, noncommitally.

Angharad stared at her.

Reluctantly she revealed her deepest fear. "I'm the only wife he's likely to have. Is it fair to be one who can't provide many children? Maybe none. We have so few, we fae, compared to what he may expect."

"But Gwyn fathered George's grandmother," Tegwen was relentless. "You'll have children with him. And they'll be raised here, not in Lludd's cursed domain like your others." She leaned forward. "There will be children in your life again, I'm sure of it."

"Our separate houses?" Angharad said, desperately.

"You'll figure it out," Tegwen said.

This was unworthy of her, Angharad thought, this grasping at straws. Enough. She straightened in her chair, and nodded to herself.

Then she flashed a smile at Tegwen. "You'll stand for me, on Saturday?"

"Of course," Tegwen said. "Who will stand for George?"

Someone cleared his throat on the other side of the doorway, and Eurig walked in, not in the least embarrassed by his obvious eavesdropping. "I will, you fool of a girl." He waggled his drooping gray mustaches at her. "I've been standing about waiting for you to talk yourself into it. Took you long enough."

Angharad stood on Daear Llosg, the ritual burning grounds north of Greenway Court, and waited at the back of the assembly with George for the ceremony to begin. She glanced nervously at Rhian in front of them. Rhian bore a silver cord and a ring, and tried not to shift from foot to foot as though she were a child instead of Gwyn's fourteen-year-old foster daughter.

That was the ring George had returned to the human world for. His grandmother had kept it, a keepsake from her own mother, Gwyn's consort. "Wife," George had corrected her, not consort. They were married by the human ceremony, and Gwyn stayed in the human world long enough to see their daughter wed after his wife's death.

She smoothed her woolen gown over her waist. It was russet, to match her loose auburn hair, enlivened with small silver and green embroidered details. She touched the thin circlet of silver oak leaves entwined in her hair.

Quit fussing, she told herself, and stole a look at George standing by her right side.

His brow was wrinkled in concentration, but he caught her glance and smiled at her. She could feel her face light up. He made a play of running his eyes down her and and widening them appreciatively, and she rolled her eyes in response. His lips quirked and he shifted his shoulders to let her critique his own clothing, his best huntsman's livery, with the wide silver groom's sash running down from his right shoulder to his left hip.

She had to admit, he did look well, broad and tall, his black hair neatly trimmed.

The weather was crisp and bright, a beautiful late autumn day. Their friends had made an aisle for them leading to Ceridwen, but she couldn't focus on their faces.

Ceridwen lifted her hand, and at that signal, the people lining the aisle raised thin oak branches, cut from living trees, over their heads so that Angharad and George followed Rhian beneath a canopy of leafless boughs.

All their friends and family were there. Weddings were simple events for the fae, outside the alliances of royalty—an excuse for festivities and a blessing, and not much more. Still, the colors on display were bright in the afternoon sunlight, as they walked slowly under the bare branches.

When they reached the front and stood before Ceridwen, Tegwen and Eurig stepped up behind them and lifted up their own boughs, a few tan leaves still clinging to the ends of the twigs.

Ceridwen looked at them solemnly. "George and Angharad, are you free to wed and do you wish to do so?"

"Yes," George said immediately.

It was uncomplicated for him, Angharad thought. He'd never been married before and had no children.

She recalled the three previous occasions she had stood in a similar place. All of those men were lost to her now, and her children from the first marriage, though living, might as well be. Still, she would do this again.

"Yes," she avowed, quietly.

"Do you swear to honor each other's children, heirs, and obligations? To share in the joys and sorrows of life, to be each other's support and delight, to live as one as long as life lasts?"

George glanced at her, with his heart in his eyes, and timed his "I do" to coincide with hers.

Ceridwen bound their hands with the silver cord she took from Rhian, her right hand to George's left. George's hand was slick with sweat, despite the cool air, and she smiled at that. You're no more used to this than I am, she thought, with your façade of confidence.

The fae ceremony was simply finished, but George turned to her with a human addition of his own. He'd told her he wanted to add something from his home. He took the ring from Rhian with his free right hand and placed it on the fourth finger of her left hand.

"With this ring, I thee wed," he intoned, and his voice thickened. "With my body, I thee worship. With all my worldly goods I thee endow."

The emotion in his voice riveted her attention. He's giving me everything, she thought. How can I do less?

He looked at her and his hand shook as he lifted his fingers from the ring on hers. He's as nervous as I am, she thought, and she laughed out loud.

To her relief, he joined her, and pulled her into a warm embrace, and a long kiss.

Ceridwen enchanted the branches along the aisles and in their sponsors' hands, and the green wood forced out new young leaves, pushing the old ones off to flutter to the ground. Angharad smelled the strong scent of spring verdure in the autumn air, and they turned to face the crowd and receive the congratulations of their friends.

Eurig and Tegwen were the first to embrace them. Whatever Eurig whispered into George's ear made him blush. Interesting. She'd have to ask him what he said.

George endured the good wishes of the attendees as patiently as he could. He learned not to look over at Angharad doing the same while he was talking with someone, because the sight choked him every time and made him fumble his words.

Looking at her auburn hair and russet dress, he felt like the world's luckiest foxhunter, to have run this one to ground.

He watched the last of the guests start their walk back to Greenway Court. Those not on foot had returned to their wagons or mounted up. There was to be a gathering there at the huntsman's house, and he didn't look forward to it, a rowdy hurly-burly of jokes and pranks intended to disturb their wedding night. It wouldn't just be a party, it would be a trial to be endured, and there was no way to escape it.

He hung back with Angharad until only the bridal wagon remained, the one that had brought her there in her fine dress. Benitoe waited up top to drive them both back, with their sponsors and Ceridwen. Before they left, everyone who had held a newly-leafed branch had affixed it upright to the side of the wagon in prepared holders, and Eurig and Tegwen had just finished adding their own on either side of the driver's bench seat, with a few pointed and ribald remarks from each of them.

Angharad seemed to be as reluctant to leave as he was. He couldn't stop smiling, just looking at her, he'd never get his fill of that. He put his right arm around her and held her close to his side, as though never to let her go.

"Do you really want to go through with the ambush at the house?" he asked her.

"Rhodri has made arrangements…," Ceridwen said. "You'll get no peace tonight."

George winced. "I can just imagine."

Angharad looked up at him uncertainly. "Could it be avoided?"

Eurig said, "Well of course it can. Many a couple before you have dodged away, refusing to be entrapped, and they'll respect you if you can pull it off. But they'll have set watchers along your trail to ensure you don't stray and spoil their fun. They'll try to fetch you back."

Tegwen said, "Rhodri's too young to deserve success every time. It would do them all good to party without you. That way it can last until morning, with no one protesting."

George glanced over at Angharad for support, and she nodded, her eyes shining.

"Those watchers will all be south of us, between here and Greenway Court," he said. "I have a plan. Will you all help?"

George and Angharad sat on either side of Benitoe on the wide seat of the wagon. The small lutin was dressed in his best red coat and breeches, and George's heart went out to him. The death of his betrothed a few weeks ago had dealt him a major blow, and today's ceremony must have been bittersweet.

Eurig saluted from the ground. The three of them would walk back, south along the road, as slowly as possible, to give the couple as much time as they could for a headstart. Eurig proposed a song, and the last thing they heard as they pulled away was his deep, jolly voice echoing down the road along the stream, seconded by two strong trebles.

What did she see in him?
Who could explain?
Another full glass,
And we'll not mind the pain.
Pain, no pain,
Again and again,
Another full glass,
And we'll not mind the pain.

Over and under him,
Country or town,
Give us one more
And we'll drink it right down.
Down, down,
Away with her gown.

Give us one more
And we'll drink it right down.

Lift up your glasses,
And do what is right.
Wish them the best,
Of both day and of night.
Night, night,
An inspiring sight,
Wish them the best,
Of both day and of night.

The dignified Ceridwen belting out a drinking song—imagine that, George thought, blushing at the words.

Benitoe turned north on the road away from Greenway Court and took them to the upper ford of the river, and then south down along the road on the other side, heading to Angharad's house in the village. They traveled in silence, for the most part, and Angharad once leaned over to Benitoe and gave him a wordless hug. The sound of the singing died away, and there were just the evening sounds and the light of the fading sun.

There was nothing to disturb them after they crossed the river, no other travelers on the village road, and George felt as if he moved through the twilight alone with Angharad. He glanced over Benitoe's head at her and caught her doing the same to him.

No smiles this time, it was too deep a feeling for that. He could sense the pull of the years to come, as though he were being rooted to this world and stitched into place. He knew he would be just an episode in Angharad's long life, he had come to terms with that, but she would be all of his. At the end of his life, she would still be there, hardly changed. He didn't understand how she could possibly consent to it, but he was beyond questioning it now. He just accepted it, with a private vow to live up to whatever she saw in him.

They turned off the road at the north end of Greenhollow and took the lane alongside her house and workshops. Benitoe drove the wagon to her back door, and George lifted out the things Angharad had brought with her for their planned night at his huntsman's house behind the court.

Benitoe said, when George had finished, "I'll go back up and cross over the ford again so that I can come down from Daear Llosg. When I drive down past the watchers, empty, that may puzzle them enough to throw them off the scent. Especially since they'll have had a few drinks by now. I think you'll get away with it."

"Tell them we're not available. I'll take the hunt on Tuesday," he said. "Maybe."

Angharad walked into Benitoe's path after he turned the wagon and stopped him. "Grab my arm," she told him, lifting it up to him. "Pretend like you've caught me."

He looked at her puzzled, but did as she asked.

"Good," she said. "Thank you for everything." She beckoned him to lean down, and she gave him a soft kiss on the cheek. He looked back as she returned to George, then drove off quietly, leaving them alone. Even her pets were up at the huntsman's house.

"What was that about?" George said.

She told him, "The bride is supposed to flee before the groom and his party. The man who catches her will marry within the year."

"Benitoe? After Isolda?" He shuddered at the memory of her death and vowed to take his own happiness while he could and not waste any time.

"It's just one of our customs," she said, "and he was the only one here."

"Ah." Like throwing the bridal bouquet, he thought. "A custom, is it? Well," he said, looking down at her, "this is one of mine."

He scooped her up in his arms and walked up the steps of the back porch to the kitchen door with her, while she laughed in surprise. His senses were full with the weight of her, the smell of her hair. He fumbled at the latch and carried her over the threshold, kicking the door shut behind him.

NIGHT HUNT

This story takes place between To Carry the Horn *and* The Ways of Winter.

His eyes popped open in the dim light cast by the banked fire. For a moment the bed felt strange and then he remembered—Angharad's house—and there she slept, turned away from him, breathing slowly. He was wide awake and on the alert.

What woke me? The snow was deep on the ground, muffling any outside noises. No cars were here to disturb him, no engines in the fae otherworld, and he was still getting used to the absence of the sounds of human civilization. He cataloged what he could hear—the tick of the embers in the fireplace, the occasional creak of the floorboards as they adjusted to temperature changes, Angharad's soft breaths.

Then it came again. Muffled barks of excitement. He looked over at his dogs by the fire. Sargent, the yellow feist, was motionless except for his chest rising and falling, but the bluetick hound was quivering in his sleep, his paws twitching as he ran. He panted and yipped, his eyes closed. No wonder it woke me, he thought.

George had no trouble providing the real sound behind Hugo's dream, the loud, deep bays as he followed a hot scent. That cry would ring off a hillside, but here it was, indoors, just a remnant to wake him in the night.

Nothing to worry about, he thought, as he relaxed back down into the warm bed by his wife's side. He wasn't sleepy, but if he stayed quiet, sleep would return.

Inevitably his mind turned to the tumult of his recent weeks. I made a choice, he thought, the most important of my life. I'll never face a bigger one. I chose to turn my back on the human world and stay here, with these new-found kinsmen.

He touched Angharad's back softly, verifying her presence. My new wife. He smiled.

It's impossible to regret the choice I made, but there are costs.

Those old-timers I used to hunt with, they knew about costs, what it was to make choices. He thought of them as old-timers but they weren't, not really. Sure, some of them were classic "ridgies," mountain types, or their fathers were, or their grandfathers. They had small houses and cabins tucked into the hollows and blue collar jobs, fixing machinery, cutting wood, clearing brush—whatever they could do to make a living and still leave time for other pleasures, especially hunting and fishing. Most were in their fifties or much older. It was hard to tell sometimes—the life they led could be hard on a man. They were lean men, by and large, though here and there one ran to fat and was teased for it by the others.

Their wives and families lived quietly, and their children mostly moved away.

They weren't all like that, of course. Sometimes a more solid citizen in the community felt the urge to join them, an atavistic need to be a part of something else, something not modern and civilized. There were always a few like that, welcomed by the night hunters because they appreciated the fellow-feeling, and because these outsiders helped them keep things afloat when times turned tough, even got them work sometimes. Their fathers and their grandfathers had known each other for as long as they could remember.

He remembered the first time he'd met the night hunters. He'd wanted to see what it was like, chasing coon and fox in the dark with hounds. He'd read what he could about it, but there wasn't much—the people who did it and the people who wrote about it had very little overlap. He'd heard more, hints from friends who always seemed to have a couple of jars of moonshine on hand. He pestered one of them, Gabriel Scott, and one moonlit October night he was invited along. Gabe warned him, "Wear clothing you don't mind losing if it gets ripped to shreds."

The two of them drove deep back into a hollow around ten o'clock. Gabe took his pickup truck up the side of the Blue Ridge along a dirt road George had never traveled before. They pulled up at an old hunting cabin where half a dozen trucks were already settled, and ten or twelve men stood around an open fire. Some had one or two dogs on leashes by their side, and he saw others in kennels in the backs of the trucks.

He knew it was a sort of audition, and he conducted himself modestly, younger at twenty-seven than everyone there. He recognized a few of them by sight. Gabe introduced him as "that young fellow, George Traherne, who whips-in for the Rowanton Hunt. Gilbert Talbot's grandson. He knows foxhounds."

"Does he, now?" Lucius Conyngham drawled. His was a quiet, sardonic sort of voice, matched to a spare body that made no unnecessary movements. His battered old fedora hat looked well-accustomed to a life out of doors. George pegged him as the leader of the group.

"I want to know what it's like, sir, how you hunt," George said. "I'm here to learn."

That sparked a jeer from some, but a nod from Luke. "Alright, then." He walked among the men and passed their names to him. Most were friendly enough, preoccupied with catching up on the news and keeping their hounds out from underfoot. They bragged on their hounds to each other, boasting about how well they'd do this time.

Most of the men had one or another type of foxhound. George thought he recognized a couple of Walkers, and there were hounds that wouldn't have seemed out of place in any Virginia pack. Not all were foxhounds, however. One scowling fellow with black hair and scraggly eyebrows held a young lanky bluetick coonhound on a lead and was being joshed by his friends. "You brought him along again? Cain't you learn?"

Gabe told George, "Hank hasn't had much luck with his hound. Too slow to keep up with the others, and we hunt fox more than we do coon."

George knew it was a point of pride which hound ran the game best, who came closest, who treed the critter first, and how their voices sang in the night.

"We all here tonight?" Luke asked. The men stopped talking and looked around.

"Looks like," one of those by the fire said.

"Let's do 'er then." Luke walked over to his truck and released two redbones from their kennels, clipping leads onto their collars. More coonhounds, George thought in surprise. They whined with excitement, and all the hounds joined in.

He counted them in couples automatically, as if they were a pack of foxhounds. There were nine couple, eighteen hounds. A mixed pack, of course, both dogs and bitches. That young bluetick was one of the tallest.

Once they all had their hounds in hand, straining at their leads, Luke looked them over. "Let 'em loose," he said, and unclipped his two. They must have hunted with each other before, George thought, for they hung together like a pack and ghosted up the slope into the dark woods out of the firelight, seeking a scent trail.

The men settled down in a semicircle on the upwind side of the fire. There were plenty of log sections set upright for seats, and they sat quietly, listening for the first cry. Most of the leaves were already off the trees, up here on the ridge, so sound would carry well.

A quart jar of clear moonshine made the rounds. When it reached George he saw a piece of fruit inside, and he could taste the faint flavoring of the peach over the kick of the raw alcohol. He sipped and handed it along, listening to the men.

They spoke quietly. One had a son in the Marines and passed along the latest news. Another had a daughter who'd presented him with his first grandchildren, twin girls. There were chuckles at that, and congratulations raised to "grandpa" as the jar went by.

A great horned owl in the woods called out with its low hoots and they hushed to listen. It repeated itself once, then stopped. Just as they started to speak again, they heard the unearthly death shriek of a rabbit, probably the owl's victim. George shuddered, and the men around the fire were quick to resume talking, to shake off the gruesome sound.

One old fellow started a tale about his son who was pestering him to come live with him down on the flats, now that his wife had been gone for some time. "I told him I just wouldn't do it. I'm fine up here, I said, I ain't leaving. Not to no goddam suburb."

They shed their children to the modern world, but chose to stay themselves. He didn't know the man, but he could picture him ten years on, dying alone in his cabin. It wasn't a sad thought, exactly—he wanted the hard life for its joys and was willing to pay the cost. He could respect that.

Except for the trucks, you could almost believe this was another century, George thought. It's a world away from my job, shiny computers and corporate customers. He shook his daytime thoughts away and focused on the men around them, how well they fit together. He didn't romanticize it, even he could see they had factions among themselves, friends and cliques, but they were united in this love of hunting and that gave them a common bond that overrode their differences. He envied them.

A clear cry rang out, upslope and some distance away. All conversation ceased, and then the sound came again, with other voices supporting it. The hounds had struck on a hot scent. They listened for a few moments and Luke said, judiciously, "T'ain't no deer. I do believe that's gray fox. My Katie don't sound like that for coon. She's partial to fox."

A deep voice joined in. "Ain't that your hound, Hank?" one of the men asked.

"Yeah, but it's coon, not fox. You wait and see."

They don't agree, George thought, watching them hide their smiles. This is an old dispute between them.

Gabe told George, "Hank bought himself a coonhound and that's what he wants it to hunt. No use telling him different."

"I love his voice," George said. It was true. The deep baying set a foundation for the chorus of higher-pitched voices.

The sounds broke off, and the men hushed, waiting. In a few moments, they picked up again, coming toward them.

"Listen to that hound of Hank's bawl." The speaker shook his head in admiration.

"My Katie's in the lead, though." Luke said with quiet pride.

George sat, surrounded by dark woods and blinded by the fire, and tried to construct a picture to go with what he was hearing. The hounds were strung out, he could tell, the deep-voiced one trailing at the end and the clear voice of the first hound to sound off still in front. That must be Luke's Katie, he thought. The voices of eighteen hounds raised in joy and eagerness resounding down through the woods was uncanny. He remembered that Washington had received a gift of bluetick hounds from Lafayette and declared they sounded "like the bells of Moscow," Now he understood what that meant, here in the dark primeval forest of his imagination.

The pack swung away from them again and went quiet. One voice raised falteringly. "That's Rebel," one man said. They listened to the hounds working out the scent, each man identifying the voice of his own hounds and supplying commentary.

"I don't know what fouled the scent," a big, testy man said impatiently to his neighbor. "If that little Hazel of yours had any sense she'd stop working tail line and point the right way for a change."

"Quiet," Luke said, and they subsided. They picked up the line again and raised the full cry once more.

"That's more like it," Gabe said, and George nodded.

The baying changed its note, growing louder and more eager, and then it stopped moving, lighting up the mountainside with joyous noise.

"Alright, boys, on your feet," Luke said. "They've treed it."

They took out flashlights, all except for a couple of the men who picked up lanterns. Luke took the lead as they picked their way up the slope, moving as quickly as they could and cursing the bushes and branches that scratched at their clothing and the rocks that turned their ankles. George was larger than most and had a harder time pushing his way through, but he was young enough to make up for it and was determined not to be a fool and get left behind to wander lost for the rest of the night.

The lights weaving up ahead of him stopped and when he reached them he saw the hounds leaping at a beech tree that still clung to its tan leaves. The trunk leaned at an angle, and several of the hounds scrambled up a few feet, only to drop off defeated. The tall bluetick was among them, George saw, baying at the top of his lungs.

The men stood by their hounds and leashed them.

"Told you it was a coon," Hank crowed, as the flashlights probed through the leaves looking for the quarry.

The beams coalesced into a single spot, and George saw the pointed nose and grizzled muzzle of a gray fox, a dog fox, he thought, not a vixen. Secure in his perch, he looked down with unconcern at the hounds below. The hounds waited for the men to take a shot and deliver him.

"Goddam you, hound," Hank hollered. "That ain't no coon." He hauled the hound to him on its lead and gave it a good kick, then picked up the lead end and started to lash him with it. The frightened hound howled and pulled himself free. He fled, trailing his lead behind him, into the dark. The rest of the hounds quieted for a moment, startled.

The men froze at the unseemly outburst. No one said a word as Hank whined, to cover his action, "I paid four hundred dollars for that hound, and I'm done with him."

George spoke up for the first time that evening. "I'll give you four hundred for him. Right now." He reached into his wallet and pulled out everything he had on him, about three hundred and twenty dollars. He waved Gabe over. Gabe handed him his wallet without a word and he helped himself to another eighty. He walked over and threw the bills at Hank's feet. "There. He's mine now. You all heard him?" he asked, looking around the ring of silent men. They nodded, and he thought he saw approval on some of their faces.

Hank leaned over and picked up the money. "I ain't helping you catch him," he said. He laughed uneasily, not liking the mood of his companions, and started back down through the woods by himself.

Luke looked up at the fox and then back at the men whose celebration had soured. "I think we'll let this one off this time, boys, what do you say?"

They agreed and headed back with their leashed hounds, moving more slowly and carefully going down than they had scrambling up. George and Gabe lingered behind.

Gabe raised an eyebrow at him.

"I couldn't let him do that, and besides, I like that hound," George said.

"You're going to have to wait for him to find his way back once he gets over it," Gabe said. "Might as well go back to the fire. That's where he'll return. If he returns."

"I know, and it might take all night. You can go on, if you want, pick me up in the morning, maybe."

"Ah, hell, I haven't got anything better to do myself," Gabe said, and they pushed their way back down to the fire in companionable silence.

When they got there, they found Hank was gone. "What're you fixing to do with that hound, if he comes back?" Lucius Conyngham asked.

"There's more to life than night hunting," George said, "though maybe this isn't the crowd to say that to. And more than coming in first."

Luke let a small smile escape him.

"Well, you could be right, at that. Someone's got to be tail hound. And he surely did enjoy himself, bawling at that fox."

"Yes, sir, he surely did," George replied.

A different moonshine jar was pressed into his hand. This one had an apple inside. He took a sip and waited a moment to catch his breath, then passed it along to Luke.

"I think we're done for the night," Luke said. "You're welcome to join us another time, son. Gabe'll let you know." He touched the brim of his hat.

"Thank you, sir. I had a fine time in your company."

"Bring that hound, or not, as you like."

They bundled their hounds into their trucks and drove off, one at a time, leaving only Gabe's truck behind. The noise of the engines and the tires on the dirt road carried for a while in the still night, but gradually died away.

"He left us a gift," Gabe said, pointing to a half-filled jar. "Something to pass the time with."

They sat next to each other by the fire, sipping away, and pausing every now and then to throw another log on to keep it alive. "You won't see that Hank again," Gabe said. "No one treats a dog like that when he's just doing his job. They won't tolerate it."

They chatted about inconsequential things in the night and watched the moon drift slowly across the sky. After an hour or so had passed, Gabe said, "Think that fool hound has enough sense to work the back trail to find his way here?"

"Probably." Hounds mostly did make their way back to where they started from when they got lost. That's why hunters left a coat behind if they had to leave. Like as not, they'd find their hound sleeping on it in the morning.

"What're you going to name him?"

"Hugo, I think. Don't know why, just seems right."

Gabe grunted and reached for the jar.

George looked up and thought he saw movement. "Hssht. Don't move."

The bluetick came tentatively out of the woods and stood outside the firelight, watching them, whining softly.

"It's alright, boy," George said in a calm voice. "He's gone. Come on in."

He kept talking, soothing the hound and patting the side of his leg. The hound circled around the fire, taking a long sniff of the log where Hank had been sitting.

"Don't you think about him anymore," George said. "You come on over and get a fuss made over you. Such a fine hound, finding that fox with the others, staying on the trail and helping them tree it. You're a good hound, you are."

The sound of the low sweet-talking voice enticed the hound all the way in, and George rubbed him all over, getting him used to the feel of his hands. He'd treated dozens of foxhounds this way, over the years, and he knew how to make a hound feel at home. "Your name is Hugo, now, and you're going to live with me."

"You do have a way with them," Gabe had said.

George smiled, in the darkness of Angharad's bedroom, as he remembered that. If he only knew, Gabe, how he could bespeak the animals now. Was that part of the same talent, then, and he didn't know it, or did that only come upon him after he crossed from the human world into this one, years later?

No way to know.

Once he'd come here, he could never have gone back. Oh, he could have walked away, it would have been allowed, but he couldn't unlearn what he'd seen. He chose to leave his old world behind, the land of night hunts and pickup trucks and moonshine. He had earned a place with those old-timers, listened to their tall tales, their stories of humor, of bravery, of fine hounds, of luck, good and bad. Most of all, of perseverance in the face of hardship, of choices made without counting the cost.

He saw them a few more times over the years, and Hugo gloried in the hunts, baying at the back of the pack like a great bell. As Gabe had predicted, he never saw Hank again.

For the last couple of years, he hadn't made the time to take Hugo night hunting, too busy with his software company. That sort of success was more facile, more about conformity and hard work than anything else. I'd had it with that, he thought. That wasn't something I needed to return to. It was his elective tribe of night hunters that he missed, and his human family, his grandparents.

But I'm back with the old-timers again, here, aren't I? Except these aren't the remnants of a proud backwater tribe, standing independent while the modern world passes them by. These are the powers in their own land. His great-grandfather Gwyn, Prince of Annwn. All the mighty fae, hundreds or thousands of years old.

Hugo's dream revved up again, and he gave little eager yips.

Go get 'im, boy. Bring him down or let him run but don't give up, don't stop.

He nodded in the darkness. *My hound will learn to hunt something else, and so will I. I'll learn to build my life here.*

He smiled. *My children will fit here seamlessly.*

He rolled over and drew his arm around his wife, holding her close, nestled up against her back. *Maybe he could dream up a hunt for himself.*

CARIAD

Benitoe busied himself with rechecking the girth on Halwyn, off to the side of the inn yard, and kept his eye on the side door of the main building. Two of the tall fae rode in and dismounted, chatting together. A groom came out of the stable to take their horses, a lutin in red like many of the staff at the inn, a foot shorter than the fae, or more, like Benitoe himself, though Benitoe wore his dark green hunt livery instead of the traditional red. The groom looked over and gave Benitoe a wave. "We've got his pony tacked up. Are you still planning to return tonight?"

"Shouldn't be any problem with that, it's just a few miles on horseback, through the ways, and the weather's clear. Do you have enough space ready?"

"Luhedoc told us to expect eight, and we can just manage it."

Benitoe took in all the construction that was still underway as the Golden Cockerel was being hurriedly restored to use. He'd seen the newest interior repairs last night after he rode in, but now, in daylight, the extent of the work was much more obvious. The stables had been in complete collapse when he'd last seen them, a few weeks ago. Maëlys had latched onto the first stone masons and carpenters to become available as the barriers dropped around Edgewood and set them to work, rightly anticipating that the reviving town would need a working inn as its dwellers came back to life, recovering from the curse that had buried them in a sort of half-life for so long.

The side door to the inn opened, and Luhedoc came out, dressed for a ride on a cold day. He walked down a couple of steps and Maëlys stopped him, pressing a leather bag into his hands. She spotted Benitoe, and smiled at him over Luhedoc's head. "Food for the ride," she called.

"Thanks, auntie." It had only been a few weeks since she had adopted him into her clan, reviving a very old custom. It warmed him still, whenever he thought of it, and he lost no opportunity to call her by the title that relationship conferred.

Luhedoc looked away into the yard as the groom brought his brown pony out of the stable aisle. "Sorry to leave while there's still so much to do, but it's as good a day as any to start bringing the horses, while they're in demand. Do you think they'll finish the laundry boilers for you today?"

"Oh, I imagine they'll come close," she said, absently. She was watching Benitoe as she spoke, and her expression made an appeal to him, as if to ask for help. She looked back at Luhedoc, but he avoided her glance.

"I'll bring back as many as I can." He turned away to check his pony, and she stood on the top step for a moment, irresolute, then walked back in and shut the door.

Luhedoc finished his inspection and fastened their lunch behind his saddle, then mounted up. "What's the name of that white gelding of yours?" he asked Benitoe as he joined him.

"Halwyn," Benitoe said.

"Of course," Luhedoc smiled. "'Salt.' Iona's stock?"

"That's right. You'll see more like him when we get there."

They left the inn yard and rode at a walk through the busy streets. "What a change," Benitoe said, as they made way for two wagons in a row and paused for a fae child, dodging around them with small regard for the hooves of their ponies.

"Is it?" Luhedoc said. "It's been so gradual, you hardly notice when you're in the middle of it every day."

Benitoe waited until they reached the edge of the small village and started up the road to the manor house. Then he drew his pony back alongside of Luhedoc and said, "What is it? What's up with you two, uncle? Is anything wrong with Maëlys?"

"Oh, she's fine. She's got that inn spinning like a top. Every day more of it comes back. She's found something that suits her talents, whatever her initial misgivings might have been."

Benitoe could hear the pride in his voice, but also a dullness. "Well, then? What's the matter?"

For a few moments, he didn't think Luhedoc would reply. Then, as they entered the manor grounds, he said, "She shouldn't have waited for me."

Benitoe was indignant. "It was very brave of her to come seek you, to find out if you were here, trapped in Edgewood."

"That's not it, of course not. I was thrilled to see her," he protested. "But eighteen years is too long. She should have married again. She deserves children and here, she's wasted all this time, waiting for me. What sort of bargain is that?"

Benitoe led the way up to the main building. The entrance to the way, opened in haste a few weeks ago, was awkwardly placed right on the terrace of the manor house itself. Benitoe saw that an earthen ramp had been hastily constructed since his last visit, so that horses and wagons could avoid the steps. The entry itself, invisible to his eyes, was marked out clearly on the stones of the terrace, and a low wall had been built on each side and behind to keep people from blundering into it from the side or rear. For the first few yards, before the transition, the start of the way occupied space like an above-ground tunnel and had to be defended from intrusion.

He had stopped talking to avoid being overheard by the guards posted at the way entrance. They knew him and waved him through, and he made sure Luhedoc was close behind him so that the way token in his vest pocket would work for them both. They rode through the dimly lit featureless passage for a few yards and felt the transition. The atmosphere changed and light from the far end illuminated the remaining yards of the way. Benitoe nodded at the guards at this end as they emerged into an open meadow by Edgewood's southern river, twenty miles south of the manor house. The entrance to the next way was about a hundred yards off, and Benitoe paused for a moment, when they were in-between the two sets of guards and out of earshot.

"You know, none of this is your fault," he said. "Be grateful you survived at all. I know she is. She talked of nothing else, the whole time we were looking for you."

"And since then?" Luhedoc muttered, in a low tone.

The whole topic made Benitoe feel queasy. The two of them had taken the place of his absent parents after years of living alone and it disturbed him greatly to see his new uncle's loss of confidence.

Benitoe took them on through the second way which cut fifty miles off their trip, leaving them just north of Greenway Court, the base of Gwyn ap Nudd, Prince of Annwn. Benitoe was a whipper-in for his hounds, the ones that ran the great hunt every year to serve justice.

Luhedoc looked up as the green living palisade that surrounded Greenway Court came into view west of the main road. Another few miles south would see them to their destination. "I think she stays with me now out of pity and I can't have that. Bad for me, and worse for her. She should have taken Brittou up on his offer years ago and forgotten about me. She'd have a family by now."

So this is what has auntie so worried, Benitoe thought. He didn't know how to convince him he was wrong. Words wouldn't do it, not between men. He wanted to say, you can't talk about giving up like that. You have to fight for what's yours. She'd want you to.

❧

They turned in off the main road and halted at the first of the large stables where the news of their arrival was carried inside by a stablehand. A middle-aged lutin strode out to greet them, wearing his red coat and weskit comfortably, here in his own place.

"Good to see you, Benitoe," he said, "and you, too, Luhedoc, at long last."

He sent one of his hands up to the estate house. "Go tell my lady Iona that our guests are here."

The two travelers dismounted and stretched after their long ride, and Brittou had two grooms run their horses in out of the cold for a bit of hay.

He came up to them, then, looking Luhedoc over carefully, and Luhedoc bristled in turn. Like a pair of gamecocks they are, Benitoe thought. Fools, the two of them—the hen already made her choice.

"So how is Maëlys faring, then?" Brittou asked.

Luhedoc did not respond right away, so Benitoe said, "My auntie's doing very well, thank you, and quite happy."

Brittou nodded carefully but kept his eyes on Luhedoc for a moment.

"Iona said to sort out six horses and two ponies for you, the horses from the herds you left behind when you went away. She said to tell you that she kept the bloodlines going after she bought them from Maëlys."

Luhedoc didn't respond to the jabs about leaving, but Benitoe was silently indignant. No one could have anticipated being trapped that way.

"I chose one of the smaller herds," Brittou said, "and put them all into a paddock for you to look over. You can take your pick from among them."

When Luhedoc finally spoke, it was to say, evenly, "Thank you for your care of what was mine, Brittou. If you don't mind, I'll ask my nephew here to choose the ponies while I start on the horses." He glanced at Benitoe to see if this met with his approval.

Benitoe let a stablehand lead him to a separate paddock area where he made quick work of selecting two exuberantly healthy young geldings, both bays, one much darker than the other. They would make fine riding stock for the fae children, or for the short korrigans who needed a temporary mount, or even the occasional lutin who liked to ride the animals as well as care for them.

His work done, he walked over to one of the main paddocks and joined Iona who was leaning on the fence. She was a small fae, small enough to ride her own pony stock. She'd taken in Maëlys as a companion when she bought Luhedoc's horses after he vanished.

"I heard about your new family connections, Benitoe," she said, smiling at him. "You've become famous."

"I'm sure auntie didn't mean for such a fuss to be raised about it," he said.

"When you revive old customs like a clan adoption, you have to expect people to take notice," she said. "It's my fault. We did a lot of reading in old books on the long winter nights."

They watched Luhedoc going over the horses on offer. The original herd was in the main paddock on the left. One at a time, Luhedoc would call out an individual horse, and Brittou and his helpers would cut it from the herd into the small paddock alongside and hold it for Luhedoc to go over. In the next paddock to the right, three horses were milling around together, watching with interest.

"Those the ones he's already chosen?" Benitoe asked.

"That's right. He wants breeding stock. I imagine he's planning to rebuild his herd over in Edgewood. What do you think of them?"

"They're native bloodlines, aren't they?" One of the young stallions was a rich bay, pale underneath, with a black streak down his back and a roached mane, while the other was a dark gray with distinctive spots on his rump. The mare with them was white with dark spots, patterned all over. They had the full-bellied sturdy form of the local horses that could run or work all day. Easy keepers, but you needed your wits about you to handle them.

"That's right. They won't stand any nonsense. Lots of opinions they have, and you must earn their respect."

The mare that Luhedoc was checking out at the moment was almost light enough to be a buckskin, with the common dark stripe and roached mane, and paler shading under her belly. He made his decision and opened the gate where she joined the other three, glad to be part of a herd again, however small.

A whinny rose from the main paddock on the left. The herd's boss mare, another all-over spotted horse with a black tail and mane, was distressed at the diminution of her herd. She neighed to the four horses in their enclosure, and they answered her. She trotted back and forth along the fence that separated her from the empty paddock and her charges on the other side.

Luhedoc came over to speak with them at the fence, his eye on the herd in the main paddock to make his next selection.

"Lovely, aren't they?" he said to Benitoe. "That boss mare, she reminds me of one from my original herd, the foundation of my bloodlines. I worked with her from before I was married, and she never failed me."

Iona said, "She's from that line, Luhedoc. That was her grand-dam."

Brittou called over from his place further down the fence, along the main paddock. "She's not part of the deal. Too hard to handle, that one, and far too useful where she is, keeping her herd in order."

Benitoe held his breath, but Luhedoc let it pass as if he hadn't heard him. Iona made no comment.

He selected two more mares, one part-spotted and one solid bay, and sent them to the holding pen.

"We're done, right?" Brittou said. He climbed the fence into the main paddock and the boss mare trotted up to challenge him. He retreated and she followed. When he stamped the ground and leaned toward her aggressively, she snorted and laid her ears back, reaching out with her teeth. The horses behind her moved uneasily, watching her.

Brittou backed up to the fence and climbed back out. "I better let them calm down for a while," he said, looking steadily at Luhedoc.

Benitoe saw Luhedoc's lip curl at this maneuver. He stood for a few moments, admiring her pacing watchfulness, then without words he took his coiled rope and opened the gate to the main paddock from the one he was in, walked through, and shut it behind him.

Without waiting for the mare to make the first move, he walked toward her purposefully. She charged him and the other horses scattered out of the way, but he threw his arms out to each side and called her bluff. She backed off and watched him, fascinated. She dodged in front of him, but he intercepted her movements, and she made a game of avoiding him.

Benitoe waited for him to pause and let her approach, but he didn't do that. Instead, he came at her steadily and confidently, constantly invading her space. He walked her in this way all over the paddock, she backing up before him, and the other horses clustering at the far end as they moved along. When another mare came up, curious, he backed her off, too, but kept his eye on the herd boss the whole time.

Finally, he stopped. The mare was backed into a corner, but calm about it, and the other horses had calmed down with her. Benitoe had thought she'd be distressed but, no, out she came to be fussed over, nickering, and Luhedoc gave her what she wanted. He ran his hands all over her and murmured in her ear, when she leaned down far enough for him to reach. Then he made a quick halter out of his rope end and climbed the fence next to her to mount her, bareback, full-sized though she was.

Iona, never taking her eyes off the scene, leaned over to Benitoe. "That's how you do it," she said, quietly.

Benitoe nodded, absorbing the moment.

Luhedoc rode her over to the corner nearest the gate and one of the hands opened it for him. He rode her through to the gate on the other side and let her in to join the other six before sliding off and removing the halter.

He called to Benitoe as he approached the fence with a spring in his step. "See, nephew? Can't let them intimidate you. They're just telling you someone has to be in charge of the herd, that's all."

He told Iona, "I'll take her, too, if you don't mind. She's very fine. I'm going to call her Cariad."

'Darling,' Benitoe muttered to himself, choking down a laugh. Brittou's inarticulate protest was ignored.

"She's for Maëlys," Luhedoc told Iona with a grin, and she nodded her approval. He went off with the stablehands to arrange lead lines and harness for the string of nine they'd be taking back to Edgewood.

Iona said to Benitoe, "She won't ride her, you know. She's not like you two."

"Doesn't matter," he said. "He will." He smiled at the thought.

Iona stood away from the fence to look at Benitoe directly. "It's good to see him back again, and none the worse for it. I was worried. He hasn't lost his touch with the horses at all."

She looked at him closely. "With Maëlys running that inn, how are they doing, will you tell me?"

"Oh, I think they'll be fine, now," he said.

THE EMPTY HILLS

This story takes place during the events of King of the May.

George Talbot Traherne turned in his saddle and checked to make sure everyone had followed him through the way without difficulty. The last time he'd brought them to the grounds of Bellemore a week ago, he'd had to cut the visit short, but this time he was determined to show them a bit more of his human world. His discovery of the fae otherworld a few months ago had changed his life and brought him a family, and he wanted to give them the opportunity to discover adventure in his world in return.

Angharad rode by his side, the new life within her not yet showing. He was nervous about her being on horseback but she'd assured him there was nothing to fear, this early. She'd had other children in her long life and he knew she was a better judge of it, but he would be a father for the first time and he couldn't help worrying.

She looked at him now, rightly judging his concern. "I'm fine," she said. "Is the weather the same in both places? It seems to me it was cloudier on the other side."

She peered up at the sky, her auburn braid touching the saddle behind her as her head leaned back. It shone against the rich blue of her riding habit.

"I don't know," George replied. "I haven't gone back and forth enough to tell. The snow cover looks the same."

Only bits of snow remained in the shady spots, most of the heavy snow of a month ago having melted in a January thaw. There would likely be more snow in February, in Virginia, but for now the ground was bare and the vegetation was locked into its winter sereness. The stands of tall pines that served as windbreaks on the estate, blocking part of the view of the main house from their location, were the only touch of green in the landscape.

George glanced back at his foster-son Maelgwn, silent on his black pony, carefully looking around at the fields and woods of

Bellemore that were visible from the caretaker's house. So much self-possession for a twelve-year old, George thought. *That hard life after his family's death has left its mark on him.*

Benitoe brought up his own pony to join George. Unlike Maelgwn, he'd been riding most of his twenty-eight years. The small lutins tended animals but riding was very uncommon for them, and Benitoe had set a new trend going.

"Thanks for bringing me along, huntsman," Benitoe said. "I was sorry we didn't have a chance at a car ride the last time."

"Well, I wanted you all to get a chance to see a bit of my world, as I saw yours."

Benitoe nodded, his eyes bright with anticipation.

Up ahead George spotted his grandparents talking with Mariah Catlett as they waited for their guests. His grandfather Gilbert stood tall and straight, watching them approach, and Georgia smiled in welcome. She'd grown up at Bellemore. It was shut up now, but she still had a personal interest in the estate.

They pulled up at the caretaker's stable. "You know the drill," Mariah said, and they spent the next few minutes putting their horses up in the stalls she'd prepared for them and removing the tack. They expected to be here for a couple of hours, at least.

George peered out of the stable door as he waited for the others to finish. His grandfather's Suburban sat in the driveway, plenty large enough for the six of them, without Mariah. George had been planning this little excursion with his grandfather for some time and was amused to recognize that his nerves were a form of stagefright, as though he were presenting an entertainment and wasn't sure what the reception would be.

Gilbert surveyed the group as they left the stable. "All ready for a trip? We've got lots to show you."

"Not too much at first, dear," Georgia demurred at his side.

George looked his little party over. Clothing—he hadn't thought of that. He'd donned some of his old human clothes from before so he would pass inspection, but Angharad in her long split skirt, deep-blue, or Benitoe in the white breeches and dark green coat and weskit of his livery as a whipper-in would attract attention. "What about their clothes?" he asked, uncertainly.

"We can give them coats," Mariah suggested, "and if they stay in the car, no one will notice." She ducked into the house to fetch suitable overgarments.

"You'll have to stick to the car, too," Gilbert told him. "You're not supposed to be here, remember."

His grandparents had helped him concoct a tale about selling his company and traveling abroad to mask his move to the fae otherworld. As a result he couldn't show his face here without raising unwelcome questions.

Mariah returned and gave Angharad one of her winter coats and provided two of her son's old jackets for Maelgwn and Benitoe.

They shrugged on the outer garments. The incongruity of the styles struck George, as though they'd wrapped themselves in dowdy clothes to dim their own brighter, more exotic ones. He'd gotten so used to the fae clothing with its faint flavor of the 18th century that it seemed normal to him and this rough masquerade in modern rags was subtly distressing.

He wouldn't let these little obstacles spoil the fun. It was a fine day for a drive.

"So how does this work?" Benitoe asked.

He finished walking all the way around the dark red car and ended up in front. As he went, he'd looked it over carefully, reaching out to touch anything that caught his eyes—the rubber of the tires, the headlights. "It's just some kind of carriage, isn't it, all made of metal. But what makes it move?"

Gilbert reached around him to open the hood, and George was amused to see the consternation on Benitoe's face when he got his first look at the myriad of parts in an internal combustion engine.

"Start it up for me, will you?" Gilbert said to George as he tossed him the keys, and George obliged, easing his bulk into the driver's seat. After putting the car in neutral with the brake set and leaving it running, he joined his grandfather just in time to hear the start of a lecture on how the engine worked.

Benitoe followed along with his eyes where the old man pointed and seemed to comprehend the basics as they were explained. "Like a clock or a mill, sort of, isn't it?" he said. "But I wouldn't know how to make even one small part of it, much less the whole thing."

On their last visit George had introduced Benitoe to electricity, and now he elaborated on the role it played in the starting of the engine, and how the engine repaid the favor by charging the battery.

"It might as well be magic," Benitoe said, shaking his head. "Think of all the things we'd need to be able to do to get to this point. Where would we start?"

"It's not that bad," George said. "We've only used electricity for the last couple of centuries, and this sort of engine for about a hundred years. That's just a few lifetimes for us."

"But that's such a short time," Benitoe said, astonished. "One person could do it all." He paused, embarrassed, "I mean, not a human."

George let it pass. "Yes, but the difference is, this wasn't the work of one man, or even a few. This comes from the tinkering of hundreds or thousands of men, over time," George said. "That's what keeps it from being easy for the fae—not enough people."

Benitoe nodded slowly, muting his initial excitement as he thought through the implications. "Not like stirrups, is it?" he said.

At George's puzzled expression he explained. "That came to the fae in the east from the human world, oh, more than a thousand years ago. Such a simple thing—it spread everywhere—but it changed all the mounted soldiers, all the ways of war."

He was suddenly abashed by his attentive audience. "At least, that's what I was taught when I learned to ride."

"No," George said, slowly, "You're right. It's not like that. Stirrups are an idea, really, that any man can implement. Cars are a whole… infrastructure. Roads, fuel—everything. I'm not sure you'd want that, or need it."

Maelgwn joined them, wrinkling his nose. "Smells strange," he said, leaning over the engine to sample some of the odors as it warmed up.

"Don't get too close and burn yourself, young man," Gilbert warned him.

Maelgwn straightened up. "It's very complicated, sir. Can it go as fast as a horse?"

Gilbert laughed out loud. "That's how we measure engines, son—in horsepower, what they can pull. I don't remember the specs offhand, but this would be a two or three hundred horsepower engine."

Maelgwn stared at him in patent disbelief, and Benitoe joined him.

"No, really," Gilbert said. "And it's not particularly powerful."

George hid a smile and left his grandfather patiently answering questions. Angharad waited with his grandmother a little distance away where they could look at the car from the side. They were chatting quietly together as he approached.

They stopped when he reached them and George raised an eyebrow.

"Just talking about family," his grandmother told him. "And names."

Angharad said, "I was telling her about the old customs, where the sons and daughters are named for their grandparents, one after another."

She smiled at Georgia. "We're slow to change, sometimes, set in our ways."

Georgia told her, "We often do the same. I was named for my mother's father, George Rice. Her name was Mary. My father told me it was her request, though we had to change it a little, me being a girl."

She turned to George. "You're named for me, you know, not for my grandfather. I was so pleased when Léonie decided to do that."

"Not Gilbert?" he teased her, gently.

"She said she'd save that one for later, that you roared just like a George when you were born." Her eyes misted up at the memory of her daughter, gone now these past twenty-four years. The other names never got used—George was an only child.

Roared, is it, he thought. He looked back at Benitoe and Mael-gwn talking with his grandfather. Everyone's finding a different thing to focus on, and not the things I would have expected. Why did I think I could control that?

Better get them into the car and on the road, he thought. That'll make things simpler for everyone.

George's grandmother assigned the seats by habit. Gilbert and she took the front seats, George and Angharad the middle row, and Benitoe was consigned to the rear with Maelgwn.

A good thing Benitoe won't realized he's been classed as one of the kids, by size, George thought. He's only about five years younger than me. Still, he was amused by the pseudo-parental seating. Nothing had changed since he was a child in a succession of his grandfather's cars.

Except, of course, that he had gotten bigger. Much bigger. Headroom was always a problem. His grandfather was equally tall, but there were more options for the driver than the passengers. Out of old habit, he took the seat behind his grandmother so that he could stretch his legs out a bit better.

He made sure Angharad was comfortable. In this very ordinary human context, with the dull brown coat obscuring her colorful clothes, he found himself struck by how still she was, how sparing of her movements. It was something he'd noticed in all the older fae and had become accustomed to. Now, here, it seemed out of place, made her seem… not human, despite the ordinary outer garment. He blinked and tried to tune out the human world, the artifacts all around him, and the familiar sense of his wife returned to him, complete with a puzzled quirk to her eyebrows as she watched his face.

When he glanced back, Maelgwn behind him seemed close enough to a human boy, a youth with curly black hair, but Benitoe gave off an air of strangeness, too, with his borrowed olive drab waxed cotton coat over his well-tailored hunt livery, dark green and frogged. What was it that gave him away as not human? His face looked like a man's, not a boy's, but then we have human midgets, or even just small men, and he didn't seem quite like that. It was the proportions, George thought. The lutin's head was just a little larger, a little deeper back to front, with the barest hint of a prognathous muzzle. His skin tones had more orange in them, less pink. If you squinted, you could imagine him turning into a fox, say, or a badger. Why hadn't he noticed that before?

Well, he thought, I'm sure everyone will look normal to me again when we get back home. People here won't think anything odd, I imagine. He reflected soberly just how disastrous it might be if he were wrong. No car accidents, he thought, please. No hospitals. I didn't think about that.

Gilbert took the driveway from the caretaker's home down to the Bellemore gates slowly, but even at twenty miles an hour it was as fast as a cantering horse and Angharad gripped the back of Gilbert's seat until she realized just how smooth the ride was.

"Everything alright, dear?" Georgia said, looking back at her.

"I'm fine," she managed, embarrassed, and George reached over and took her hand.

A glance at Maelgwn revealed the universal teenager's love of speed, and Benitoe echoed that exhilaration right back.

After Gilbert reached the gate of the estate, and turned right onto the tree-lined country road, he brought the speed up to forty-five and, for the first time, an approaching car at the same speed swooshed by. There were stifled exclamations of alarm, and all three of George's guests braced themselves for possible collision.

"We keep to one side of the road," Georgia hurriedly said. "See the line down the middle? That way we don't hit each other."

I should have warned everyone about that, George thought.

More cars passed in the opposite direction, and they quickly got used to it. George caught his grandfather's eye in the rearview mirror and gave him a half-smile of chagrin. They seemed to be thinking the same thing—maybe this wasn't such a great idea after all. Too late now, he thought.

The woods and fields began to give way to farms and small old homes as they approached the outskirts of Rowanton.

The passengers were quiet, taking it all in, until Angharad spoke up. "The houses are mostly made of wood, aren't they? Not stone. I like those porches."

George hadn't thought about how many of these older houses had porches on two stories, sometimes on both the front and the back of the building, to catch whatever breezes were available in the hot Virginia summers. Sleeping porches, they were, for staying cool at night.

Maelgwn said, wonderingly, "Every house has a car or two. Is that instead of horses? They must be very rich."

Benitoe's face echoed the same question, and George said, "Most horses are used for pleasure now, not necessity. Everyone has cars. It's not because they're rich, it's because cars aren't very expensive. An old, used car might cost, oh, say two month's wages for a poor man. They last for years, and maintaining them is cheaper than keeping a horse, by and large."

He saw the surprise in Benitoe's face and added, "We make cars with machines and we make a great many of them. That makes them cheaper. If we had to build each one by hand, as you do for a carriage, they would be much more expensive. And fancy ones cost more, naturally."

"Sad," Benitoe said, "a world with few horses."

George hoped for more enthusiasm when they finally reached the town.

They bumped over the railroad tracks and rolled down the main street of the little village. Rowanton wasn't much larger than Greenhollow, just enough for three long streets, several cross streets, and a few stores. The Southern States feed store was prominent, right after the tracks, and then a drugstore, two small restaurants for pizza and burgers, and the post office. A convenience store at the gas station stood in for a grocery—the next town was large enough that most folks did their serious shopping there.

George thought of it as quaint and sleepy, but now his unease made him look at it as his guests might. There were lights everywhere, he realized, even in the daytime. Georgia described what a stoplight was and what the colors meant as his grandfather came to a halt at the one light in town.

Angharad cleared her throat and asked, "How do they make those signs?"

What signs, he wondered. She pointed at the branding on the commercial buildings, the business names in colorful plastic, the bits of elderly neon signage still visible in some of the storefronts.

"Um, different materials, plastic or metal. The lit signs, well, there's a gas that glows colorfully when you run electricity through it…" He wound down in the face of her bafflement. "I'll explain later."

Over her shoulder George's grandmother said to him, "Maybe we'd better turn around, dear. Enough for one day, don't you think?"

He nodded, wordlessly, and Gilbert drove around the block to leave town the way he came in. As they approached the railroad tracks, the crossing barriers began to drop and the train warning lights and dongs went off.

Oh, no, I haven't told them about trains yet, he thought. Hastily, he said, "Don't be alarmed. There's a metal rail on the ground and huge machines, like giant cars, run on that track and pull, um, wagons behind them. Very big, very noisy."

And, he forgot to tell them in time, very fast. A typical long distance freight train rumbled through at a good clip, three diesel engines in front pulling an endless string of freight cars.

The ground shook under the car which trembled in place only fifteen feet from the grade crossing, and Angharad's face froze. Maelgwn had the car door open before George's warning penetrated and he paused, half out of the car, looking to escape. "It's alright," George insisted, kicking himself as he tried to calm them. This was such a bad idea, he thought.

He watched them take hold of their alarm and settle back down. It took several minutes for the hundred or so cars to pass, and Benitoe recovered enough to try and make a joke about it. "Is that what you have instead of ways, huntsman? How does it stop?"

George silently blessed him for being more interested than scared, or at least acting like it, but he feared Angharad didn't feel the same.

"I'm sorry, dear," he said. "I didn't expect we'd see a train or I'd have warned you."

She smiled shakily. "Oh, it's just a bit startling," she said. "What would that be like, I wonder, running down the middle of Greenhollow?"

"Noisy," Benitoe said, promptly.

"Smelly," Maelgwn added.

"And dirt everywhere," Angharad capped, the three of them united in a moment that excluded George.

There must be some way to salvage this, he thought, make them see the wonder of a different world without scaring them half to death.

The strangeness of their surroundings was much reduced as they retraced their journey over now-familiar ground, and the mood inside the car gradually recovered after the shock of the train. The visitors stared at a distant view of hay being cut by a sickle-bar mower and Benitoe commented, thoughtfully, "How very much work that does, but how very hard it would be to make one."

"Only if you make them one at a time, from scratch," George said. "A farmer can rent the machine, or buy it, or share it with his neighbors. It's part of the cost of producing his crop, just like draft horses would be. Not far from here, there are farmers who don't approve of machinery who use horses instead." He thought of the Amish and Mennonite farmers in the remoter parts of the county, then shook his head at the notion of trying to explain religious dissenters and anti-modernism. Though perhaps his guests would sympathize, he reflected, with a quirk of his lips.

Angharad seemed to be mesmerized by the forms of the houses. When he tilted his head and looked at her, she elaborated, "Your people fit their dwellings into the landscape differently, don't they."

It was true, he thought. Even the best sited of the older houses lacked that sense of being part of the land that was so common to the fae dwellings, the ones not in towns. "Remember, we've only been settled here for a few hundred years ourselves. It takes time…"

A shadow flitted over her face, and he knew she was thinking of the difference in their lifespans, the likelihood that he would have an ordinary human life and be soon gone from her, by fae standards. He patted her hand and smiled reassuringly. He was reconciled to it, if she was not.

It struck him then—what would the landscape look like if Greenhollow and Greenway Court weren't there, the way it was before the fae settled. "Grandmother, could you hand me the maps in the glove compartment?"

Gilbert glanced back at him. "What did you have in mind?"

He selected the one he was looking for from the handful she gave him. "I wanted to see…" He spread out the local one on his lap, located Bellemore, and then searched west from there, along the Blue Ridge. "Yes, this must be it. Grandfather, do you think we could take a little detour?"

"Why not? Where to?"

"I'm searching for a place that overlooks the Pocosin State Forest," he said, staring at the map. "If you'll go out towards Harvey Bennett's place, and then onto the West Kirtle Mountain Road, I think there's a spot."

He turned towards his guests and gestured enthusiastically. "I want to show you one last thing, something you'll all recognize." He could give them a glimpse of their home from the other side, something he'd wished for himself when he'd first crossed over.

Angharad smiled gamely.

❧

The view from the steep drop-off up on Kirtle Mountain that looked west to the Blue Ridge was everything George had hoped for, and the state had created a small pull-out alongside the gravel road to honor it. Since no one else was around to see them, they all took the opportunity to get out of the car and stretch.

"Why did you bring us here, huntsman?" Benitoe asked.

"Can't you tell? Look, you see that notch on the ridgeline? The way the little stream drops down and joins the larger one running along the base of the ridge? What does that remind you of?"

The uninterrupted winter forest along the eastern slope of the Blue Ridge marched for miles north and south, with no obvious roads through it visible from this spot. It must be like traveling back in time for Angharad. She'd been in the first wave of fae settlers almost 1500 years ago. He waited eagerly for them to realize what they were looking at.

I wanted adventure, he thought, and I found it, over there, with the fae in their version of my world. The least I can do is return the favor and show them my side.

Maelgwn spoke up. "That's the notch above Daear Llosg, isn't it? It's not cleared over here, it's still forest. See, if you trace the stream down," pointing, "that's where the bridge at Greenhollow would be." His voice trailed off.

Benitoe said, "And Greenway Court would be there, I suppose," looking at the unbroken woods across from him on the upslope.

George looked over at Angharad in the silence. Her hands were shoved deep into the pockets of her borrowed coat. She glanced up at him and pointed with her chin. "My house in the village would be right there, wouldn't it? There's nothing there, over here, nothing at all." There was desolation in her voice.

He looked in dismay at his grandmother and the unspoken reprimand in her face struck him full force. This isn't what he'd meant to happen at all.

"Such empty hills," Angharad murmured, and shivered. "As if we had to start all over again."

He laid his hand on her arm and cleared his throat. "I'm so sorry, my dear. I thought you would enjoy this." Selfish, he chided himself. They weren't looking for annventure, for an escape from the mundane. That was my wish, not theirs. I should never have subjected her to this—she's not Benitoe, younger even than I am. Her whole long life is there, and all her work. It's where she's rooted herself. I've shaken those foundations, showing her this.

She leaned against him, rallying. "Never mind. I've learned some very interesting things today. This isn't a perspective I could ever have anticipated, and I'm glad to have seen it."

"So clumsy of me," George said, ruefully. "This wasn't what I wanted to do." He put his arm around her and turned her toward the car. "Let's go home," he said, "all of us."

GUIDE TO NAMES & PRONUNCIATIONS

MODERN WELSH ALPHABET

A[1], B, C, CH[2], D, DD[2], E[1], F[2], FF[2], G, NG[2], H, I[1], J,
L, LL[2], M, N, O[1], P, PH[2], R, RH[2], S, T, TH[2], U[1], W[1 2], Y[1]

[1] These letters are vowels. The letter 'W' can be used either as a vowel (when it is said 'oo' like in the Welsh word 'cwm' (coom) meaning 'valley') or as a consonant (when it is said like it is in English, for example in the Welsh word 'gwyn' (gwin) meaning 'white'). This is the same with letter 'I' which can also be used as a consonant (when it is said like an English Y like in 'iogwrt' (yog-oort) meaning yoghurt).

[2] Letters that are not in the English alphabet, or have different sounds. CH sounds like the 'KH' in Ayatollah KHoumeini. DD is said like the TH in 'THere'. F is said like the English 'V'. FF is said like the English 'F'. NG sounds like it would in English but it is tricky because it comes at the beginnings of words (for example 'fy ngardd' - my garden). One trick is to blend it in with the word before it. LL sounds like a cat hissing. PH sounds like the English 'F' too, but it is only used in mutations. RH sounds like an 'R' said very quickly before a 'H'. TH sounds like the 'TH' in 'THin'. W has been explained in the sentences before about vowels.

It helps to remember how Welsh is pronounced in order to translate the unfamiliar orthography into familiar English sounds. The language has changed over time and so has the spelling. People with very long lives tend to be conservative in how they spell their names.

Some nicknames are descriptive, occupational, or locational, as they are in English (e.g., Tom Baker, Susan Brown, John Carpenter, Meg Underwood)

Bongam - Bandy-legged
Goch - The red(-haired) one
Owen the Leash
Scilti - The thin one

PRINCIPAL CHARACTERS & PLACE NAMES

HUMANS

Conrad (Corniad) Traherne
Father of George Talbot Traherne, husband of Léonie Annan Talbot.

George Talbot Traherne
Huntsman from Virginia. His parents are Conrad Traherne and Léonie Annan Talbot.

Georgia Rice Annan
Mother of Léonie Annan Talbot, wife of Gilbert Payne Talbot, daughter of Gwyn ap Nudd (Gwyn Annan).

Gilbert Payne Talbot
Father of Léonie Annan Talbot, husband of Georgia Rice Annan.

Léonie Annan Talbot
Mother of George Talbot Traherne, wife of Conrad (Corniad) Traherne.

Mariah Catlett
Human agent for Gwyn ap Nudd and George Talbot Traherne. Lives at the caretaker's house at Bellemore.

FAE & IMMORTALS

Angharad (ang-KAR-ad)
Artist affiliated with Gwyn ap Nudd's court.

Beli Mawr (BEH-lee MA-oor) - Beli the Great.
Father of Lludd Llaw Eraint (Nudd) and Llefelys.

Brynach (BRIN-akh)
Great-nephew of Eurig ap Gruffyd.

Ceridwen (ke-RID-wen)
Scholar, healer, magician at Gwyn ap Nudd's court.

Cernunnos (ker-NOO-nus) - Master of Beasts.

A god who takes the form of an antlered man (the horned man) or an antlered red deer-man.

Edern ap Nudd (EE-dern ap NIDH)
Son of Lludd Llaw Eraint (Nudd), brother of Gwyn ap Nudd and Creiddylad ferch Nudd, father of Rhys ab Edern, grandfather of Rhys Vachan ap Rhys and Rhian ferch Rhys.

Eurig ap Gruffydd (EI-rig ap GRIFF-ith)
Father of Coronwen. Husband of Tegwen, great-uncle of Brynach. Vassal of Gwyn ap Nudd.

Gwyn ap Nudd (GWIN ap NIDH) - Gwyn Annan.
Son of Lludd Llaw Eraint (Nudd), brother of Edern ap Nudd and Creiddlyad ferch Nudd. Father of Georgia Rice Annan. King of Annwn.

Iolo ap Huw (YO-lo ap HUE) - diminutive of Iorwerth.
Huntsman to Gwyn ap Nudd.

Iona (YO-na)
Breeder of ponies and small horses.

Llefelys (lhe-VEE-lis)
Son of Beli Mawr. Brother of Lludd/Nudd. Uncle of Gwyn ap Nudd, Edern ap Nudd, and Creiddylad ferch Nudd. Husband of Coronwen ferch Eurig. King of Gaul.

Lludd Llaw Eraint (LHIDH LHAU er-AYNT) - Nudd/Lludd of the Silver Hand.
Son of Beli Mawr. Brother of Llefelys. Father of Gwyn ap Nudd, Edern ap Nudd, and Creiddylad ferch Nudd. King of Britain.

Maelgwn (MYLE-goon)
Young way-finder, friend of Granite Cloud. Adopted son of George Talbot Traherne.

Nudd
See **Lludd Llaw Eraint**.

Rhian ferch Rhys (HRII-an verkh RHEESE)
Foster-daughter of Gwyn ap Nudd, daughter of Rhys ab Edern and Eiryth, granddaughter of Edern ap Nudd, sister of Rhys Vachan ap Rhys. Junior huntsman to Gwyn ap Nudd.

Rhodri ap Morgant (HROD-hrii ap MOR-gant)
Distant cousin to Gwyn ap Nudd, cousin to Rhian ferch Rhys and Rhys Vachan ap Rhys. Diplomat and way-finder to Gwyn ap Nudd. Musician.

Rhys ab Edern (HREESE ab EE-dern)
Son of Edern ap Nudd, husband of Eiryth, father of Rhian ferch Rhys and Rhys Vachan ap Rhys.
Rhys Vachan ap Rhys (HREESE VAKH-an ap HREESE) - Rhys the younger, Rhys Junior.
Foster-son of Gwyn ap Nudd, son of Rhys ab Edern and Eiryth, grandson of Edern ap Nudd, brother of Rhian ferch Rhys. Earl of Edgewood under Gwyn ap Nudd.
Tegwen (TEG-wen)
Mother of Coronwen. Wife of Eurig ap Gruffydd.
Thomas Kethin (KETH-in) - Thomas the Swarthy.
Son of Thomas, Lord Fairfax, and Dilys

LUTINS (LOO-tanh)

Benitoe (BEN-ih-toe)
Whipper-in. Nephew by adoption of Maëlys.
Isolda (i-SOL-da)
Daughter of Ives, betrothed to Benitoe. Deceased.
Ives (EVE)
Kennel-master. Father of Isolda.
Luhedoc (LOO-eh-doc)
Husband of Maëlys.
Maëlys (may-EL-iss)
Wife of Luhedoc, runs the Golden Cockerel inn in Edgewood. Aunt by adoption of Benitoe.

HORSES

Brenin Du (BREN-in DII) - Black King.
Pony for Maelgwn. Black gelding.
Brittou (BRIH-too)
Stable manager to Iona.

HOUNDS - CŴN ANNWN

Cŵn Annwn (COON AN-nun)
The Hounds of Hell. See **Annwn**.

Gwennol (f) (GWEN-nol) - Swallow.

DOGS (OTHER)

Hugo
A blue-tick coonhound owned by George.
Sergeant
A yellow feist owned by George.

PLACES

Annwn (AN-nun)
Part of the Celtic otherworld, traditionally the underworld. See **Cŵn Annwn**.
Daear Llosg (DEI-ar LHOSK) - Burnt Ground.
The meadow on the slope north of Greenway Court where funerals and cremations are held.
Llys y Lon Las (LHIIS eh LOON laas) - Greenway Court (Court of the Green Lane).
The name of Gwyn ap Nudd's manor, later borrowed (before 1750) by a human visitor, Thomas, 6th Lord Fairfax, as a name for his wilderness estate and hunting lodge at White Post, in the Shenandoah Valley.
Pant-glas (PANT-glaas). Also **Pantglas**. - Greenhollow.
The name of the village below Greenway Court.

IF YOU LIKE THIS BOOK…

MORE GOODIES

You can find **more information** and illustrations of George's pocket-watch and the oliphant at:
KarenMyersAuthor.com/link-bound-into-the-blood/.

Continue reading for an **excerpt** of the first chapter of **The Chained Adept**, the first book in **The Chained Adept** series, and find out more about it here:
KarenMyersAuthor.com/link-the-chained-adept/.

Don't forget the remainder of the series **The Hounds of Annwn** which you can read about here:
KarenMyersAuthor.com/link-the-hounds-of-annwn/.

Sign up for the **newsletter** to stay informed of new and upcoming releases and to get occasional bonuses, like free short stories:
KarenMyersAuthor.com/signup.

Let other readers know what you think by leaving them a review where you bought the book.

CONTACTING THE AUTHOR

You can contact Karen Myers at KarenMyersAuthor.com or by email at KarenMyers@KarenMyersAuthor.com. You can also follow her on Facebook: Facebook.com/KarenMyersAuthor.

ALSO BY KAREN MYERS

The Hounds of Annwn

To Carry the Horn
The Ways of Winter
King of the May
Bound into the Blood

Story Collections
Tales of Annwn

Short Stories
The Call
Under the Bough
Night Hunt
Cariad
The Empty Hills

The Chained Adept

The Chained Adept
Mistress of Animals
Broken Devices
On a Crooked Track

Science Fiction Short Stories

Second Sight
Monsters, And More
The Visitor, And More

See KarenMyersAuthor.com for the latest information.

EXCERPT FROM THE CHAINED ADEPT

The Chained Adept: 1

Available from Karen Myers and Perkunas Press

Penrys was crouched on one knee, slamming the *rysefeol's* recalcitrant wooden joint with the back of her hand by way of a delicate adjustment, when the sudden transition hit.

"Oh, *thennur holi*," she said, under her breath, but the oath that started in her well-lit workroom finished in swaying light and strong shadow. Already off balance, she tumbled on her backside. The soft surface took the sting out of it, and her hands, spread wide to break the fall, told her of carpet and, below that, uneven ground. A gust of wind blew smoke in from outside and the walls fluttered.

A tent, she realized, and a very large one.

She saw the people, then, and froze, stifling a sneeze, but they didn't seem to have noticed her. *No, that's not it. They aren't moving at all.*

Perhaps no one's moving but someone's talking. She tilted her head and pinpointed the voice—it came from something like a mirror suspended from a metal stand in front of the nearest tent wall. She was too close alongside the same wall herself to see anything but the edge of the frame.

The flickering light from the glass-enclosed lanterns on the tables and chests in the tent cast moving shadows on the faces of the people. It gave the illusion of life, distracting her for a moment, and then the words from the voice in the mirror penetrated.

"…a field test like this is always useful for a new weapon. I look forward to greeting you in person, when you arrive for a permanent visit."

She wrinkled her nose at the lazy baritone drawl. *That can't be good. What's happened to them?*

Glancing over her shoulder, she spotted a red lacquered chest along the tent wall and scooted back a couple of feet to set her back against it, taking care to stay out of the line of sight of the mirror. She crossed her legs and made herself comfortable on the rug, licking her dry lips as she tried to focus.

She steadied her breathing, then, and reached out with her mind to the people in the tent with her. She could only see a few of them from her position on the ground, but her mind told her there were seven. All the minds projected fury and fear, but one shone more clearly, aware of her, and able to respond silently when she focused on him.

Who are you? No, never mind. Can you help us?

That gave her pause.

What have we got here? Something from the mirror, smothering them all like a thick fog. But not me—probably doesn't know I'm here. At least, not yet.

She braced herself, and then raised a mind-shield around the one who'd asked for help. Immediately she felt the force shift and bear down upon her, but she diverted it around them both and let it flow away.

Much better. What about the others?

She judged the force that beat at her. *Maybe one or two more.*

The Commander, then.

Penrys couldn't drop her concentration long enough to look for him. *Show me.*

He gave her the flavor of the other man's personality and indicated a direction. That matched up with one particular mind, and she extended her shield to him.

The lights dimmed for her as she took on the load. She closed her eyes to remove the distraction and listened to the muttered conversation in the tent.

"What...?"

"Not now, Commander-chi. Temporary defense. Pick one more man."

Silence for a moment.

"Make it Kep, then."

This one, please. Her first contact pictured another personality and direction for her, and she extended the shield one more time, hoping it would hold.

She gritted her teeth and focused on the task. At least the load was steady—she could bear the pressure for a little while, if it didn't change. *Why so few? I should be able to support more of them. But it doesn't feel like that would work just now.*

"I'm not sure what you hoped to accomplish, Menbyede, but I think you may have misjudged our strength. Kep-chi, see to the men and prepare for attack." She recognized the voice of the second man.

"At once, Commander-chi."

The air shifted as someone left the tent.

The voice in the mirror was quiet, but the force increased against her shield, probing and shifting. She strengthened the shield further, clenching it solid, until the sounds outside dropped away.

A finger tapped Penrys's shoulder and the familiar mental voice that marked a wizard followed. **You can stop now.**

Cautiously, she loosened the shield enough to look, and found the pressure gone. Her whole body ached as she released the shield completely, and she slumped to loosen her muscles, her dark shoulder-length hair falling into her face as she rotated her head and felt the neck joints crack.

"You didn't hear me speak to you," the man said, his deep, resonant voice low and private against the bustle behind him in the tent. He crouched next to her on the balls of his feet.

Sandalwood? She sniffed again and lifted her head. The honeyed voice belonged to a smooth-shaven Zan traveler, his hair concealed under a small maroon turban. His dusky robes of an overall small-figured fabric had been shortened for ease of movement, and his loose breeches were bloused over decorated but well-worn leather boots. He regarded her soberly, and then his dark eyes widened. He reached out and pushed back her hair on one side to confirm his glimpse, exposing her ear—her shaggy, mobile, fox-like ear.

She jerked her head back and staggered upright. Glaring down at him, she shook her hair loose again to cover her ears.

He rose more gracefully and made her a sketchy half-bow. "Your pardon, *bikrajti*. I was just... surprised."

Penrys looked beyond him and realized the tent was large and multi-part, four square bays surrounding a central square, the ties at the corner seams marking its origin as five separate structures. It was dark in the corners but full of activity. *Uniforms. So, I was right—this is a military camp. But where?* Her companion seemed to be the only Zan—none of the rest, bare-headed or not, showed the loose curly hair she would have expected. To a man they had short, straight, black hair, and several cultivated wispy beards. A glance out of one doorway confirmed that it was still nighttime.

A courier had arrived and was reporting to Commander Chang, easily identified by both his voice and his location—anchoring a wide camp chair, fronted by a large, portable table, little of which was bare of papers, and commanding a view of the tent entrance, where an armed man stood ready on either side. A quick glance confirmed that the mirror was gone from the stand by the tent wall.

The dark Zannib wizard followed her gaze. "Locked away it is, where it can do no more harm." He paused. "We *think* it can do no more harm."

"I'm called Zandaril," he said. "We must talk, soon as he's free." He cocked his head over at Chang.

He drew her over to the Commander's table and they waited for the courier to complete his report. The smoky cressets outside the tent flap still held the night at bay, but the clamor of a roused camp belied the darkness. Voices called back and forth, and hoofbeats pounded by. As Chang leaned forward in his chair for emphasis, it creaked and his black leather jerkin reflected the candle light dully.

Once Chang had dismissed the courier, he turned his full attention to Penrys. His lined face was impassive, the eyes narrow.

"Who are you? What just happened? And how, exactly, did you happen to turn up, in such a… *timely* way?"

It was clear from his face and the tone of his voice that he didn't believe in coincidence.

"It's complicated, sir." She cleared her throat. "There was an accident…"

At the sound of her northern Ellech accent, Chang's eyes met Zandaril's. The Commander and the rest of the men in the tent, with the exception of Zandaril, had the look of the eastern Kigali folk, their eyes tightened against the ancestral wind and their beards sparse.

She forged ahead. "M'name's Penrys, and I was in Tavnastok a little while ago. But not now, I think."

"No." Zandaril blinked. "Indeed not. It's far from the Collegium you are, way up in the valley of the Mother of Rivers." At her blank look, he added, "Near the western border of Kigali."

Penrys closed her eyes briefly and shook her head. *Thousands of miles if it's a step, as much south as west. What have I done? How will I get back, with nothing but the clothes I stand in? How can I tell them at the Collegium where I am?*

She studied the two faces before her, one stern, one curious. *Well, that may not be my most urgent problem. They think I had something to do with this attack.*

She straightened up. *First order of business—stay alive and out of prison.*

Penrys waited in Zandaril's company while the Commander made certain that the threatened attack was not about to materialize, based on the reports of his returning scouts as they continued to come in.

She glanced at her oh-so-polite custodian. *It's not like I can go anywhere, from the middle of an armed camp. That they know of, anyway. Guess they don't see it that way.* In spite of herself, she yawned and belatedly covered her mouth.

At Zandaril's raised eyebrow, she protested, "I've come west a great distance, so my night just got a lot longer."

She left it at that, not wanting to admit that the shielding had also had its cost. *And just why did I have to stop at holding three under my mind-shield? Where did that limit come from?*

"Who was in the mirror?" she asked him, quietly.

"Menbyede of the Rasesni."

"I've read about them—they're your neighbors to the west, aren't they? Who's this Menbyede fellow?"

He narrowed his eyes at her suspiciously, without comment

"No, I don't know," she said, answering the unasked question. "Hey, I can name several colleagues from the Collegium who will vouch for me and where I was last night. Um, this night."

"And what should we do with you while we wait for messages to go and return, all the long way?" Zandaril said. "Or perhaps you have a better means of communication?"

His eyes slid to the spot where the mirror had been.

She swallowed and decided to resume her silence. As if to contradict her resolve, the smell of the hot, bitter *bunnas* sitting untouched on Chang's crowded camp table made her stomach growl, audibly. She was always hungry after a prolonged effort, but it was food she wanted, not that foul stuff.

That's not actually a bad idea, though—using a mirror to cross distances. How did they attach sound to the vision? How do they focus it? How far can it go? And how do they send an attack through it, like the one I shielded?

She settled down to ponder ways and means, her fingers itching for something to write on.

With the camp on high alert until daybreak, but no enemy detected, Chang finally returned his attention to her. Two of his officers stood behind him and waited. She could feel the suspicion radiating off of them.

"I would like an explanation," he said. It was little short of a command.

May as well tell them part of the truth, anyway. Not that they're likely to believe it.

"I was at my workshop, at the Collegium. Working on my…" She paused. "You see, I made this *bendu*, a device, kind of a detector, a *ryskymmer*, like a bound-circle, only the reverse…"

They looked at her blankly. *These are Kigaliwen, and they don't have the terms.*

She started over. "Look, if you take a defined space, like a big box, you can cancel out the magic inside the space." She framed the concept out with her hands.

She glanced at Zandaril. He was nodding as if he'd heard of the theory.

"Most people stop there," she said, "but I thought if you could set it up right, you could use it to find active magic somewhere else."

Zandaril stopped nodding, but she pushed on anyway. "And if it's big enough…" She spread her arms wide to illustrate. "You could maybe go where that magic is." *If you were fool enough to stand on the inside of it.*

There was silence for a moment, broken only by the spitting of the cressets outside.

"What, seven thousand miles?" Zandaril raised both eyebrows this time.

"Well, I had it set up to look for the biggest activity it could detect. I didn't think it would go further than the Collegium. After all, there's plenty there for it to find. And besides, I wasn't trying to use it—the full-scale version wasn't working yet."

Didn't think about what I was doing. Idiot.

Zandaril said, "So the Rasesni tried out their new weapon, and…"

"It sucked me in. I was on the inside, tinkering with the framework's joints, but then I, um, hit it and, wham, here I was."

She could feel her cheeks heating. "Guess it worked."

Zandaril and Chang exchanged opaque looks.

Chang began again. "You sound like a Northener, but you don't have the look."

"No. No, I don't." She cleared her throat. "About three years ago, they tell me, there was a disturbance out in the forests of Sky Fang in the Asuthgrata region, enough to bring Vylkar, the local wizard, out to track it down."

"You?" Zandaril suggested.

"Well, I'm what they found." She raised a hand and fingered the heavy chain resting high around her neck like a collar.

Waking up at the base of a rough-barked tree, surrounded by torches and strange, armed men. Waiting for them to speak and then tapping them for the language.

"And where had you come from? How did you get there?"

"Wish I knew. That's all there is, nothing further back."

"But you knew the language?" Zandaril asked.

She compressed her lips. "I know all the languages. I get them from the speakers."

She looked at them pointedly. "Yours, too, you may have noticed."

Chang glanced over at Zandaril for confirmation, and Zandaril shrugged.

"I've never heard of that," the Zan remarked.

"Yes, that's what Vylkar said. It's true, nonetheless."

He let it pass, though his skepticism was plain on his face.

"So, you ended up at the Collegium."

"They figured it was the best place to… examine me. They gave me a name and a bunch of tests." She half-smiled. "Then they argued a lot."

"You're what, then? An apprentice? A *nal-jarghal?*" Zandaril asked.

She snorted. "No, they couldn't really make me fit properly anywhere in their system. Old Aergon declared they should revive the ancient title of *hakkengenni,* um, 'Adept.' All I wanted was a place to work, and to persuade them there was no harm turning me loose in the library. Help 'em with the catalogue."

"And they did? They just took you in and exposed everything to you? The Collegium, with its reputation for stringent qualifications?" Zandaril snorted.

"And what's the first thing you did, eh?" Penrys said, and cocked her head at the corner where she'd arrived. "Tried to find out what I was and what I could do, didn't you? You're no different then the rest of your wizardly colleagues."

She heard her voice rise. "Made m'self available for experiments, I did. That was the exchange. Made some devices, too, not that they're any too eager to use 'em. Why? You want to come up with some tests yourself?"

"Enough," Chang said, and she subsided.

"Sorry." *Don't be a fool. Don't alienate them—they may be your only means of getting back.* She took a deep breath, and sneezed from the smoke of the cressets drifting inside.

"Whatever the Rasesni had in mind seems to have been called off. I'm going to stand down the camp." Chang waved over one of the guards at the entrance.

"Take our… guest over to Jip-chi and have her assigned quarters for what's left of the night." He glanced at her. "Under guard, if you please."

Zandaril stroked his beardless cheek as he settled back in the folding camp chair and watched Chang's face. The quiet discussions elsewhere in the tent gave them a bit of privacy. "What did you think of her story?"

"She has to be a Rasesni plant," Chang said. "Nothing else makes any sense. Accent or not, she's certainly no Northener, not with that dark hair. Not skinny enough, either. Or tall."

"She is what, then? Who are her people? Not the bandy-legged Rasesni." Zandaril let that hang there for a moment.

Chang nodded, reluctantly. "No. Not a pure-blood anyway. Probably some sort of border family, mixed-blood. Or something else."

"I know what I saw." Zandaril shook his head. "I don't know any border families with pricked animal ears, Commander-chi. Do you? Not even in the old granny tales."

Chang glared at him. "You have a point?"

"You should believe her story for now, as long as it doesn't disturb your mission."

"And what's to keep her from vanishing the same way she materialized?"

Zandaril had been facing that corner of the tent when he was locked in place by the Rasesni attack. He'd seen her arrival, tumbling on her rear with her arms flailing. *That was the clumsiest entrance I've ever seen. Hard to associate that with a secret enemy.*

He poured himself a mug of the still-hot *bunnas*, lifted it to his nose, and inhaled before taking a sip. "If she needs a large device to travel, as she claims, we can prevent it. If she lied about it, and needs nothing, how could we stop her?"

"Chains," Chang said, with a frown.

Ah, yes, I want a closer look at that necklace she keeps fingering. I didn't recognize the style.

He put the mug down on the ground beside his chair.

"I'll take charge of her," he said.

"What, in Hing Ganau's wagon? And won't *that* start rumors."

"Oh, come now, a young girl she is not, Commander-chi."

"As if that mattered." Chang narrowed his eyes. "She's young enough, and I didn't hear mention of a husband. Still, the idea has some merit—who better than you to defend us if she's not what she says?"

He thought for a moment. "All right. If she can ride, we'll mount her, else she can bounce along in your traveling warehouse with the rest of the odds and ends. Think you can catch her if she makes a run for it?"

Zandaril raised one robed arm and let the sleeve flutter gracefully while his hand waggled in the air. "Outride me she will not."

"Then she'll be in your charge tomorrow. You've just made yourself responsible for her."

Well, I asked for it, did I not?

ABOUT THE AUTHOR

Karen Myers is a fantasy and science fiction author, best known for her heroic fantasy novels.

After a degree in Comparative Mythology from Yale University and a career as an industry pioneer building software companies, she has devoted herself to writing speculative fiction. Her stories feature heroes in real and imagined worlds filled with magic, space travel, and adventure.

When she's not writing, she enjoys hunting, fishing, photography, and playing her fiddle.

Karen lives with her husband, dogs and cats in an old log cabin in the mountains of central Pennsylvania, surrounded by wildlife. Bears, coyotes, deer, and possums visit often, and when she fiddles on her porch, the wild turkeys talk back.

She can be reached at KarenMyers@KarenMyersAuthor.com.

www.ingramcontent.com/pod-product-compliance
Lightning Source LLC
Chambersburg PA
CBHW071012120726
47910CB00004B/1493